CC

Meet Maya

Chapter 1: The Expedition Kicks Off, So Let the Fun Begin!
Chapter 2: Traversing Through Tricky Terrain
Chapter 3: Yakety-Yak Adventures & Whirling Wonders
Chapter 4: Conquering the Yeti's Turf
Chapter 5: Sky-High Surprises & Lake Larks
Chapter 6: Rebuilding with Guts & Giggles
Chapter 7: Farewell to the Peaks: A Himalayan Heart's Journey

About the Author

COPYRIGHT

Maya's Yeti-licious Himalayan Hike / A Treksy Tale
Published by South Node Publishing

Edited & Illustrated by Condor Publishing

Published & Printed in Great Britain

ISBN HB: 978-1-0686618-6-0
ISBN PB: 978-1-0686618-2-2
ISBN E-PUB: 978-1-0686939-0-8

MAYA'S YETI-LICIOUS HIMALAYAN HIKE: A TREKSY TALE

MAYA'S WORLDLY WONDERS

SHARIKA CHAUHAN

Edited and Illustrated by
STEVEN MOORE AND TOULLA CORTI AT
CONDOR PUBLISHING

SOUTH NODE
PUBLISHING

MAYA'S WORLDLY WONDERS

Based on the inspiring true stories of a British Indian girl's thrilling adventures and captivating journeys, where she shares tales of compassion, courage and clumsy calamities.

A GENTLE WARNING

ATTENTION, FEARLESS ADVENTURERS!

This book is your ticket to thrilling escapades and daring exploits across incredible countries!

But remember, safety first! While our brave character conquers risky challenges, it's important to understand that the author can't take responsibility for any mishaps or boo-boos that might occur if you try these adventures solo. For maximum fun and safety, team up with a grown-up guide!

And hey, just so you know, any shout-outs in this book doesn't mean the author is giving a thumbs-up to any specific tour, gang or company, or how they roll.

And remember, intrepid explorers…

Buckle up, stay sharp and let the adventures begin!

FROM THE AUTHOR

To all the brave, intelligent and curious young girls and boys out there—venture forth and explore the beauty of our world!

Sharika Chauhan

MEET MAYA

Unleashing the Curious Explorer Within

Meet Maya, a pint-sized dynamo of exploration with a soul full of dares.

Maya is not your average Indian girl; she is a bold and intrepid explorer with a spirit as wild as the mountains she dreamed of conquering one day.

In a world where the ordinary fades, Maya stands out like a dazzling star. Imagine her: a spirited Indian girl, her petite and curvy frame brimming with an adventurous spirit. Her brown skin, kissed by the sun, is a canvas waiting to be painted with tales of wonder. And her hair? A cascade of shimmering golden-brown that dances in the wind as she embarks on her next escapade.

However, Maya isn't your typical traveller. She's a true adventurer—a born leader who explores the uncharted corners of each country she visits. Forget mere selfies in front of famous landmarks; Maya immerses herself in the heart of each destination. She forges connections with locals, unravels mysterious secrets and becomes a modern-day ninja on a daring mission.

And let me assure you, Maya doesn't spin her tales from thin air.

They're genuine, authentic accounts of pulse-pounding moments and breathtaking discoveries. Buckle up, because her escapades will leave you perched on the edge of your seat, wide-eyed and breathless.

Maya's Roots: From the London Bustle to Global Wanderlust

Throughout her childhood in the suburbs of Greater London, Maya's experiences were far from the norm. Maya forged a strong bond with her Hindu parents, who were immigrants from India and East Africa, during tumultuous times. Their resilience and courage became the foundation for Maya's aspirations of faraway lands and daring escapades. As she stargazed and caught comets in her fantasies, her audacious spirit took flight, inspired by the tales her parents told.

Epic Odyssey: Passport Stamps and Footprints

Maya's wanderlust knows no bounds. With over 40 countries stamped in her passport, her footprints span wide distances, extending from the breathtaking peaks of the Himalayas to the sun-kissed shores of southeast Asia. Inspired by her grandfather's legendary tales of traversing continents via every mode of transport imaginable, and guided by her parents, who instilled a streetwise savviness into Maya, she uncovers their mysteries with confidence and resilience.

India: Where it All Began

Maya's exploration kicked off with a leap across the seas to the enchanting land of India. Its vibrant colours, bustling markets and ancient temples welcomed her with open arms. From the majestic Taj Mahal to the serene backwaters of Kerala, India kindled the flame of adventure in young Maya's heart. Thus, her journey began, spanning the globe and leaving lasting imprints.

More than a Globe-Trotter: Maya's Flavourful Palette

Maya isn't just about sightseeing. She's a self-proclaimed foodie with an insatiable appetite for spicy cuisine—even if it leaves her sweating!

Sunsets are her secret rendezvous, and city cycling fuels her adrenaline.

Beaches and mountains? She's at home in both. And her collection of travel memories? It's a treasure trove of recollections, filled with ink-stained pages and sketches of exotic places.

In school, Maya's a math whiz, crunching numbers as if they were a breakfast cereal. She finds herself torn between equations and expeditions. However, she embraces both, ensuring her love for travel adventures aligns with her passion for numbers!

Chasing Dreams: Maya's Unwavering Resolve

Sure, she stumbles, and sports aren't her forte. But Maya refuses to let anything deter her. Life's twists and turns? She faces them head-on, like a seasoned explorer. Because, my fellow adventurers, Maya has learned that practice makes perfect.

So, grab life by the chopsticks, slurp up every moment, and dive headfirst into this wild, wacky and whimsical adventure we call existence!

READY TO JOIN MAYA ON AN EPIC ADVENTURE?

LET'S DIVE IN!

Thorong-
Ma
Anna
ci
Poon Hill

ass
Pisang
purna
cuit
Dharapani
Tal
Bhulbhule
Kathmandu
Pokhara

1

THE EXPEDITION KICKS OFF: LET THE FUN BEGIN!

DAY ZERO

At the pinnacle of the Annapurna circuit lies the mighty Thorong-La pass (Thorong Phedi), about 125 miles west of Mount Everest, the highest mountain in the world! It's like a vast, awe-inspiring quilt spread over the landscape!

But as Maya's journey approached, her nerves jittered, making her resemble a jumble of jumpy frogs. Maya had seen on the news that a colossal earthquake had recently jolted the entire country of Nepal.

As Maya arrived at Heathrow Airport, her backpack brimming with excitement and her heart pounding with anticipation, she crossed her fingers and toes, hoping that Mother Earth had finished her seismic shenanigans. She was on a mission to explore the majestic valleys, scale the lofty peaks and navigate the rugged slopes of the *Annapurna* massif.

During her journey, she aimed to mingle with the village locals and extend a helping hand to communities still piecing themselves together after the earth-shaking event.

Arriving in the humid air of Kathmandu

city, Maya laced up her hiking boots, eager to hit the trails and trek along the towering Annapurna Himalayan circuit to conquer the highest pass in the world.

As Maya joined a seasoned crew of explorers in Kathmandu, her excitement soared like a shaken soda, gearing up for the 21-day expedition that lay ahead. But just when she thought nothing could dampen her spirits, she overheard two of her fellow trekkers whispering, *"She doesn't look like a real trekker to me. I bet she won't last a day."*

It wounded Maya's pride, but she wasn't about to let a few doubters dishearten her.

"Oh, just you wait," she muttered under her breath, her determination burning brighter than ever.

Despite her petite frame and limited experience, having only climbed the Snowden crests in Wales with her family, Maya was determined to prove them wrong, one rugged step at a time.

2

TRAVERSING THROUGH TRICKY TERRAINS

DAYS 1-8

An anxious Maya set off on her trek with her brand new but very squeaky backpack, gaping at the kaleidoscope of rich landscapes unfolding before her.

Hiking the circuit anti-clockwise, from the tropical and alpine forests in Tal to the jagged highland peaks in Dharapani, each step brought her closer to the core of the Himalayas. To Maya, it almost felt as if she were going back in time. But as she and the team climbed higher and higher, the temperatures plummeted faster than a clumsy penguin on ice skates, leaving the whole group bundling up in three layers of clothing to stay toasty.

After indulging in a delicious bowl of rice, dhal and lip-smacking momo dumplings, she would curl up in her snug sleeping bag. To combat the cold, she would use her flask filled with hot water as a makeshift heater.

Despite the bone-chilling cold and the gnarly terrain, Maya's determination never melted away. She was determined to overcome whatever challenges lay ahead, fired by her boundless curiosity and unshakeable spirit for travel expeditions.

As Maya bunked down for the night in her cozy hut, some unexpected guests joined her... the silent and friendly house geckos, happily munching away on insects in the corners. Although Maya couldn't avoid feeling spooked by their scuttling, she was so tired from all the walking that before she knew it, she was out like a light and fast asleep!

In the early hours of the morning, Maya's trusty guides would stir her from her deep slumber, bringing a steaming cup of ginger tea. The spicy brew instantly awakened Maya as she prepared to tackle another day of steep foothills. However, there were mornings when Maya received unexpected wake-up calls.

Once, while brushing her teeth at the outdoor sink, she encountered a mammoth black spider, the size of her face, dangling from its web in front of her. With toothpaste still foaming in her mouth, Maya bolted back to her room faster than a shooting star, declaring, *"No thank you!"*That creepy-crawly encounter was four legs too many for Maya to handle!

3

YAKETY-YAK ADVENTURES AND WHIRLING WONDERS

DAYS 9-14

As Maya trekked through the craggy Himalayas in Pisang, she stumbled upon some quirky companions—yaks! These fluffy beasts grazed in mountain meadows, their horns shining like prizes in the sunlight. Maya found it impossible not to giggle at their comical faces and clumsy antics.

But the real odyssey began when Maya faced the challenge of crossing the long and wobbly canopy bridges suspended high across the deep chasms. With each stride, it seemed as if she and the gang were dancing on a tightrope, her heartbeat racing faster than a caffeine-fuelled cheetah.

With colourful prayer flags fluttering all around, Maya channelled her inner acrobat and gracefully hopped, skipped and jumped across the bridge with a helping hand from her fellow trekkers, reaching the other side unscathed.

And who could forget the orange-robed Buddhist monks in Manang performing their daily rituals atop the holy temples? Maya observed in awe as they meditated, feeling a wave of peace envelop her like a refreshing light breeze, with the magnificent silhouette of the Annapurna range as the backdrop.

Outside the temple, the natives of Nepal spinning the sacred wheels fascinated Maya. They circled the stupa (dome-shaped shrine) clockwise, as if they were contestants on a game show, with each whirl sending good vibes.

Amidst the crowd, an old man paused beside a statue, his fingers dancing with meditation beads as if they were playing hopscotch. With a serene smile, he pressed his palms together and lifted them to his forehead, unleashing the sacred chant of *'Om Mani Padme Hum',* as if casting a mystical spell.

His moment of peace lasted as long as a Snapchat streak, but its impact lingered like the aroma of incense sticks.

Inspired by his tranquility, Maya joined the spiritual parade, her guides and sherpas in tow.

Maya sought blessings and protection with a prayer on her lips and a skip in her step. She hoped to reach the Thorong-La summit in peak condition and conquer whatever the Himalayas threw her way!

4

CONQUERING THE YETI'S TURF

DAYS 15-17

At long last, Maya faced her ultimate challenge—tackling the daunting climb to the Thorong-La Pass, the granddaddy of all mountain passes and the loftiest pass in the world!

Maya and her companions slowly trudged up the steep, snow-covered slopes in the wee hours of the morning. Her heart raced, her breath formed frosty clouds and her legs protested with every uphill step. Doubts crept into her mind like mischievous snow fairies, teasing her with questions of her skills. *Can I actually do this?* she pondered, her fingertips tingling from the icy chill.

But with the hearty cheers of her companions and the uplifting chants of the sherpas and guides, Maya summoned her inner warrior and pressed onwards. She refused to let a few naysayers rain on her parade! And to fuel her determination, she scoffed her last chocolate bar with gusto, ready to master the peak with a sugar-powered spirit!

When Maya finally reached the summit, she leapt for joy like a kangaroo on a trampoline, her heart ascending above the surrounding peaks. Tears of triumph streamed down her cheeks as she soaked in the breathtaking vista of snow-capped cones stretching as far as the eye could see.

"I knew I could do it and prove my fellow trekkers wrong!" she exclaimed with a grin that outshone the sun.

With cheers and high-fives galore, Maya and her trekking buddies formed a huddle, bouncing with excitement like popcorn kernels in a hot pan, celebrating their epic victory!

Even the trekkers who said she would never last a day shouted, *"You did it! We will never doubt you again!"*

Standing at 4,516 meters above sea level, Maya experienced a sense of being on top of the globe—for just a few seconds, she was literally the highest person on the planet!

Maya stood proudly atop the summit, basking in the glory of her triumph, unable to resist the overwhelming sense of gratitude towards her faithful guides and sherpas. These mountain mavens were the unsung heroes of the majestic Himalayan range, navigating the treacherous terrain with bravery and finesse.

With more monster climbs than *Spider-Man's* web slinging sessions, they led Maya and her gang to victory, their strength and endurance akin to *Iron Man*.

Moving everyone's cargo like Hercules, they raised bundles of gear onto their heads and shoulders, making it seem like a piece of cake. Maya was awestruck by their unwavering kindness and resilience, feeling as humbled and inspired as a kitten meeting a lion.

As Maya slogged back down the steep, ice-covered slopes early in the afternoon, the crazily high altitude was finally taking its toll, and her bladder felt like it was about to burst.

Feeling sickly, and desperate for relief, she remembered there were no toilets on the mountaintops. With no other choice, Maya plopped down in the snow, her bare bum contacting the chilly snow.

"Talk about a frosty reception!" she joked to herself, as her stomach roiled like a washing machine while experiencing an immense sense of relief as she finally found comfort.

5

SKY-HIGH SURPRISES AND LAKE LARKS!

DAYS 18-20

Maya's antics continued as she strapped on her wings and took to the skies to fly from Poon Hill to Pokhara. Imagine zooming over the rocky mountains in a teeny-tiny aircraft, with your tummy doing somersaults as if you were riding on the big dipper. Soaring through the fluffy clouds, Maya felt invincible, like a mission-bound champion!

And the fun wasn't over yet!

Next on the agenda, Maya set sail on a serene boat trip across the crystal-clear waters of Pokhara Lake, with the oars as her faithful companions. Picture the massifs mirroring their magnificence in the glistening emerald waters below, like a magical painting come to life. Maya felt as if she were in a fairy tale, cruising through paradise with her friends.

As Maya disembarked from the boat in Pokhara, a bustling scene of tourist shops, food stalls and rosy-cheeked children greeted her, creating a warm and inviting atmosphere.

Amidst the commotion, a vibrant magenta-pink blanket called silently to her from a nearby stall, beckoning her with its colourful charm. But, upon closer inspection, she discovered that someone had crafted the blanket using yak wool! Reflecting on her past interactions with the mischievous yaks in the highlands, Maya experienced a twinge of guilt and sadness, choosing to forego the souvenir.

From creepy eight-legged bumps to high-flying escapades, Maya's trek through the Himalayas was anything but ordinary.

6

REBUILDING WITH GUTS AND GIGGLES

DAY 21

Having completed the circuit, and now back where her adventure started in the lively heart of Kathmandu, where the sun blazed hotter than a dragon's breath, Maya's heart swelled with awe at the unstoppable Nepalese spirit. After the devastating earthquake, Kathmandu faced a pickle. Maya witnessed the locals' impressive rally to restore order. Inspired by their resilience, Maya knew she had to jump into action.

Maya's adventure wasn't over yet!

So, with her trusty trekking team by her side, Maya dove headfirst into the realm of construction at a local school. Armed with bricks and cement, they tackled the task like a team of superheroes saving the day.

"Let's restore this place so these kids can hit the books again!" Maya said, bubbling with enthusiasm. As they sweated under the scorching sun, Maya couldn't help but beam with pride at the thought of making a real difference.

Amid the sweat and hustle, the local kids entertained Maya and her crew with a hilarious lunchtime spectacle. Their side-splitting charades performance kept their morale soaring higher than a kite!

However, just when Maya thought the day was a wrap, her stomach performed its own symphony of strange noises.

"Uh-oh," Maya muttered, sensing nausea. It seemed the infamous *Delhi belly (bad stomach ache)* had paid her a most unwelcome visit! Maya felt as if the hands of a giant Yeti were gripping her stomach and squeezing, though she knew it must have been something she'd eaten. It reminded her to be a little more careful what she chose for her next delicious meal.

Regardless of her woozy state, Maya soldiered on, determined not to let a pesky bellyache ruin her day. After all, even a bout of belly blues couldn't dim her sparkle.

With each brick laid and each giggle shared, Maya's bond with the Nepalese people grew stronger. Together, they proved that laughter truly is the best medicine—even for a case of the belly wobbles!

7

FAREWELL TO THE PEAKS

HOMEWOOD BOUND

A Himalayan Heart's Journey

When Maya's Yeti-licious Himalayan hike reached its finale, a whirlwind of emotions hit her that rivalled the most chaotic amusement park ride!

Maya had felt from the start that this journey would change everything. She stared down towering peaks, battled icy winds and even went toe-to-toe with some serious judgment—not to mention wrestling with her own inner fears of self-doubt!

But guess what? With every single step, Maya did more than just conquer the mountains.

It wasn't just the breathtaking views or the race to reach the highest pass that left Maya feeling as if she had hit the jackpot. Maya understood that adventure meant more than just visiting landmarks; it encompassed the incredible journey itself.

The heart-pounding challenges, the triumphs with her trekking team and the many compassionate moments were unforgettable.

Every day turned into an interactive learning adventure. From the resilient Nepalese community rebuilding after the earthquake, to the trekking gang and sherpas who became like family, and the curious and cheeky kiddos she helped at the local school.

Yep, for Maya, adventure extended beyond mere locations. It was about the people she met and the memories they shared.

As she gazed out at the horizon, she whispered to herself, *"Until next time, Himalayas. For now, let's follow the wind and see where it leads!"*

Oh, and of course, not before digging into one last mouthwatering plate of rice and dhal, complete with an extra side of momo magic!

And so, my fellow explorers, as Maya's frosty ride ends, always remember that the most incredible escapades are out there, waiting for someone as daring as *you* to grab hold of them!

So, buckle up those boots, dive into the unknown like a fearless cannonball and let your imagination blast you over heights you have only ever daydreamed about.

And hey, here's a secret: do not let anyone rain on your parade!

You are the master of your destiny, a superhero in your own story!

So, adventurer-extraordinaire, squeeze every last drop of fun out of every single moment!

Dhanyabād (Thank you), *Nepal.*

The End

DID YOU ENJOY YOUR ADVENTURE WITH MAYA?

THEN YOU'LL LOVE THESE TOO.

MAYA'S WHIMSICAL JAPANESE JOURNEY

Get ready for a giggle-packed adventure with **Maya's Whimsical Japanese Journey!**

Scan the QR code or type the URL into your browser to buy:

Http://geni.us/Japan

MAYA'S MARVELLOUS MALAYSIAN QUEST!

Embark on a whirlwind escapade with **Maya's Marvellous Malaysian Quest!**

Scan the QR code or type the URL into your browser to buy:

Http://geni.us/Malaysia

ABOUT THE AUTHOR

Once upon a time, Sharika wasn't always diving into the realm of children's books. Nope, she used to be knee deep in the wild world of financial services in jolly ol' London. But then, BAM! Something magical happened, and she realized her true calling lay elsewhere.

So, off she went, flinging herself into all sorts of cool experiences. She became a mentor for young whippersnappers at The Prince's Trust, a bigwig trustee for a charity, and a cheerleader for kids who struggled with reading.

Now, let's talk about her family. They're like something out of a storybook themselves! Her grandparents were from India, and they made an incredible voyage to East Africa to help build a ginormous railway. From there, they hustled up a storm, starting a shoemaking business that rocked. Talk about determination!

Then her folks decided it was time to trade the African adventure for a British one, fleeing the craziness of Uganda and Tanzania. Yup, things were chaotic back then with this dictator named Idi Amin running the show.

But through all the twists and turns, Sharika found solace in her imagination. She'd daydream about epic lands and far-off escapades, planting the seeds of her passion for exploration.

And speaking of adventures, Sharika's had her fair share! She's trotted through over 40 countries, from the towering peaks of the Himalayas to the sandy shores of southeast Asia. Along the way, she's gulped down each spicy dish and relished every moment, spinning tales that'll make your heart skip a beat.

Sharika created Maya's Worldly Wonders to honour her own intrepid journeys, and now she hopes to inspire young girls and boys like ***you*** to embrace your own bold steps into and around the world.

Printed in Great Britain
by Amazon

50336829R00044